The Tiny Kite of Eddie Wing

◆

by Maxine Trottier
paintings by Al Van Mil

A CRANKY NELL BOOK

KM Kane/Miller Book Publishers
Brooklyn, New York & La Jolla, California

To William, and the kite we fly together
　　Maxine

To Annette, with love
　　Al

First American Edition 1996 by Kane/Miller Book Publishers
Brooklyn, New York & La Jolla, California

Originally published in Canada in 1995 by
Stoddart Publishing Co. Limited, Toronto

Text copyright © 1995 by Maxine Trottier
Illustrations copyright © 1995 by Al Van Mil

Library of Congress Cataloging-in-Publication Data

Trottier, Maxine.
The tiny kite of Eddie Wing / by Maxine Trottier ;
paintings by Al Van Mil. -- 1st American ed.
Summary: Too poor to buy a real kite, Eddie flies an
imaginary one that catches the attention of Old Chan,
the wealthy patron of the kite festival.
[1. Kites--Fiction. 2. Imagination--Fiction.
3. Chinese Americans--Fiction.] I. Van Mil, Al, ill. II. Title.
PZ7.T7532T1   1996   [E]--dc20   96-3100
ISBN 0-916291-66-9

Printed and bound in Singapore by Tien Wah Press Ltd.
1 2 3 4 5 6 7 8 9 10

Grateful acknowledgment to Chiang, Chiu Sum
for permission to use Chan's Poem on page 24
(translated on back cover).

Once there was a small boy named Eddie Wing. He lived in a city of tall hills by a bay. His home was above a flower stall and each day he helped his parents at their work. His mother and father loved him very much, but they worried over him. From the moment Eddie got up until the moment he went to sleep, he thought of nothing but kites.

Like most of the people on their street, the Wing family was very poor. Though Eddie could dream of fine silk kites, there was no money for even the smallest paper kite. So, Eddie made do with his dreams.

Every day after the flower stall was closed, Eddie Wing would climb to the top of the city's highest hills. There, he would run through the grass holding an imaginary string in one hand. With the other hand he would pull on the invisible cord and urge a kite that only he could see up into the cold, blue sky. At first the other children laughed. Then they stopped to watch. Finally one day, they all ran behind Eddie, cheering for the kite that they could *almost* see.

Eddie's favorite event of the year was The Festival of Kites. He had watched the competitions ever since he could remember. And ever since he could remember, a prize had been offered by Old Chan. Chan was the most prosperous man in the whole neighborhood. He owned a large restaurant and a store. Everyone who passed him in the street stopped and bowed.

Of course, Old Chan no longer worked in his restaurant. He only sat outside the store and thought about the days before he was so important — when he was a little boy in China with his whole life ahead of him.

In those days he had his own dream. He had wanted to be a poet. But when his family sailed across the sea to make a new start, there was no time for poetry. Chan's dream lay hidden like a tiny seed that has been planted, but never watered.

It was Chan who made up the test for The Festival of Kites each summer. One year it was for the fastest kite. Another time it was for the kite with the longest tail. No one knew from year to year what challenge Old Chan would set before them, but as the days grew longer and warmer, he could be seen sitting in the sun outside his store, thinking.

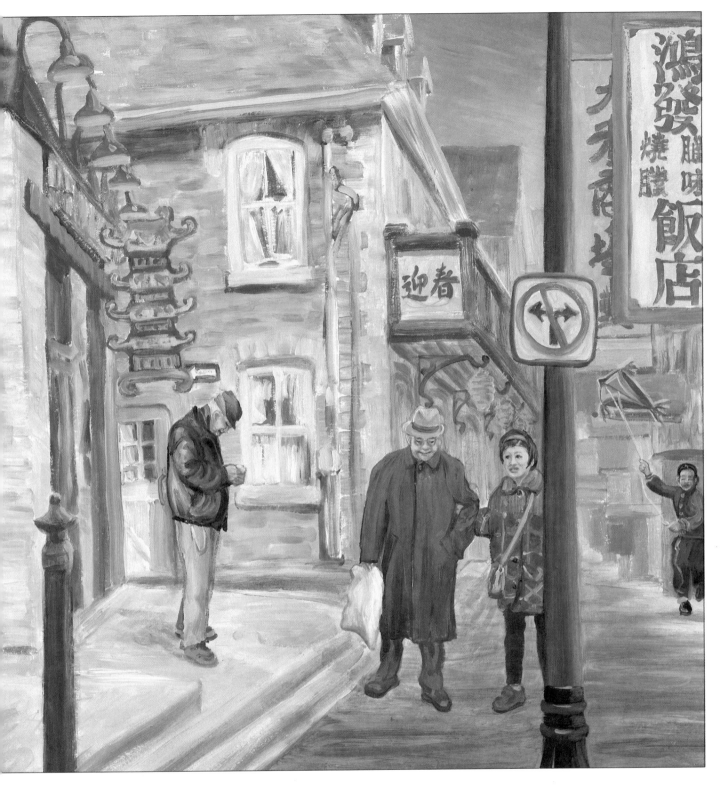

"He is deciding about The Festival of Kites," everyone would say, and sometimes he was. But more often than not, he made up small, secret poems inside his head, poems he never wrote down.

Eddie Wing could barely sleep the night before Old Chan announced this year's challenge. When he closed his eyes he saw colored shapes drifting in his small room above the flower stall. All night long the snap of kite tails filled his ears.

Finally morning came, and as he always did, Old Chan announced his challenge.

"This year," he said, "the prize will not be for the fastest kite. It will not be for the biggest kite, or the one with the longest tail. This year the prize can only go to the kite that is smaller than any other." Then Chan sat back down to enjoy the sun and to doze. Before he slept, he made up a secret poem about tiny flying things. Unwritten, it drifted about in his sleepy head before floating away forever.

At once, people began working on their kites. They bought thin cord and short, light sticks. Those who could not afford silk bought brightly colored paper.

But Eddie did not even have the money for that. Each day he helped his parents
with the flowers, and each afternoon he climbed the tallest hill in the city. There,
with all the other children running behind him, he flew his dream kite.

On the day of The Festival of Kites, the sun shone and a fine, strong wind blew just as it should. With Old Chan leading the way, everyone climbed to the top of the highest hill. One by one, the people launched their kites until the sky was filled with swooping color.

Each kite was smaller than the last. Tiny jewels of silk and paper shivered and danced in the sunlight. It seemed impossible that such delicate things could hold together in the wind, but Old Chan knew they would.

Then Chan noticed Eddie. "That boy," he said. "What is that boy doing? He is flying an invisible kite." For off a little way from everyone else ran Eddie Wing with the other children behind him.

At first all the people laughed as the boy urged his dream kite higher into the sky. Then they stopped and watched. Later on, some of them admitted to their friends that they *might* have seen something tiny and bright and clear riding high in the sky over the bay.

Old Chan knew better. He gave the prize to a girl who had flown a very small kite indeed. It was amazing that such a tiny seed of a thing could catch enough wind to fly.

But, as everyone walked back down the hill to eat and drink at the festival, Old Chan beckoned to Eddie. "Come with me," he said.

Together, they walked through the streets to the door of Chan's store. They went inside, and after much digging and moving and crinkling of paper, the old man handed Eddie Wing a parcel.

"Yours was a very tiny kite; too small to actually see. You know, you must try to do something about that."

Eddie began to open the parcel, but Old Chan stopped him. "Run along, boy: I feel a poem coming on."

When Eddie got home, he opened the parcel by himself. In the stiff, red paper lay a length of silk, some light sticks, and a ball of cord.

A few days later across the highest hill, all the children were running behind
Eddie Wing once more. Now though, his kite could be seen by everyone, and it
was a beautiful kite indeed.

空空兩手有誰憐
舉頭家望鄰紙鳶
何來錢幣備紙線
爺娘無錢買紫米

As for Old Chan, well, he went back to his chair in the sun. In his head he made up a poem about the little boy who flew a tiny kite of dreams, a kite of air as small as a seed. But this time, before the poem could float away, Chan took up a brush and wrote it down.